FLOCK

*For Jody,
Maya and
Layli*

Brimming with creative inspiration, how-to projects, and useful information to enrich your everyday life, Quarto Knows is a favourite destination for those pursuing their interests and passions. Visit our site and dig deeper with our books into your area of interest: Quarto Creates, Quarto Cooks, Quarto Homes, Quarto Lives, Quarto Drives, Quarto Explores, Quarto Gifts, or Quarto Kids.

Text and illustrations © 2019 Gemma Koomen.
First published in 2019 by Frances Lincoln Children's Books,
an imprint of The Quarto Group.
The Old Brewery, 6 Blundell Street, London N7 9BH, United Kingdom.
T (0)20 7700 6700 F (0)20 7700 8066 www.QuartoKnows.com
The right of Gemma Koomen to be identified as the author and illustrator
of this work has been asserted by her in accordance with the Copyright,
Designs and Patents Act, 1988 (United Kingdom).
A catalogue record for this book is available from the British Library.
ISBN 978-1-78603-204-1
The illustrations were created using gouache, ink and coloured pencil
Set in Baskerville
Published by Rachel Williams
Designed by Zoë Tucker
Edited by Katie Cotton
Production by Kate Riordan and Jenny Cundill

Manufactured in Guangdong, China CC022019
1 3 5 7 9 8 6 4 2

FSC
www.fsc.org
MIX
Paper from
responsible sources
FSC® C001701

Gemma Koomen

FLOCK

Frances Lincoln
First Editions

At the edge of the woods there is a great tree.
Peep through the branches and you might just
see some little people who stand as tall as your
thumb and have heads the size of hazelnuts.

They are the Tree Keepers.

If you look very closely,
you'll see the Tree Keepers busy
working together. They polish the
buds, harvest the fruit and
collect the dew.

Nurture and mend,
gather and tend,

that's what Tree Keepers do.

But Tree Keepers have fun too!
You'll see them playing catch the acorn,
twig tag and tug the vine.

Well, you might
not see everyone
doing that...

You probably won't notice Sylvia at all.
She likes to be alone,

looking for the right-shaped twig
or petal to put in her basket.

Sylvia brings these
treasures back to her little hollow.
Here, she plays her favourite games
for hours, out of sight of the
other Tree Keepers.

It's her special secret place.

But one wild
and windy
spring day,

Sylvia finds
someone
else there!

"This place is taken," says Sylvia. "You'll have to go."

But the baby bird just chirps loudly.

Sylvia reaches out to stroke its soft, scruffy feathers.

"I think you're lost," says Sylvia.
"I'll look after you."

"What's your name, little Scruff?"
"Scruff," copies the chick.

Scruff takes a little bit of getting used to.

He is noisy,

and messy,

and *always* hungry.

But he's also sweet and chirpy and loves to play Sylvia's games.

The new friends do everything together,

but there's one thing Scruff can do that Sylvia can't.

"Wait!" says Sylvia. "I want to fly too."

Sylvia looks at the drop below.

It's scary but she holds on
tight and closes her eyes…

Whoosh!

Up here the world looks different, bright and breathtaking.

All day long, Scruff and Sylvia explore new places.

They eat new things and meet new friends.

As the light begins to fade,
Scruff soars into the sky.
What has he seen?

These new friends look just like Scruff!
He chirps happily as he swirls and twirls with
the other starlings. Sylvia holds on tight!

"Careful!" she says to Scruff, but he just flies
faster and faster with the others, until...

"Wow!" says Sylvia.

As the flock of birds swoops and loops together,
thousands of wings beating as one,
Sylvia realises something.

Scruff isn't lost any more.

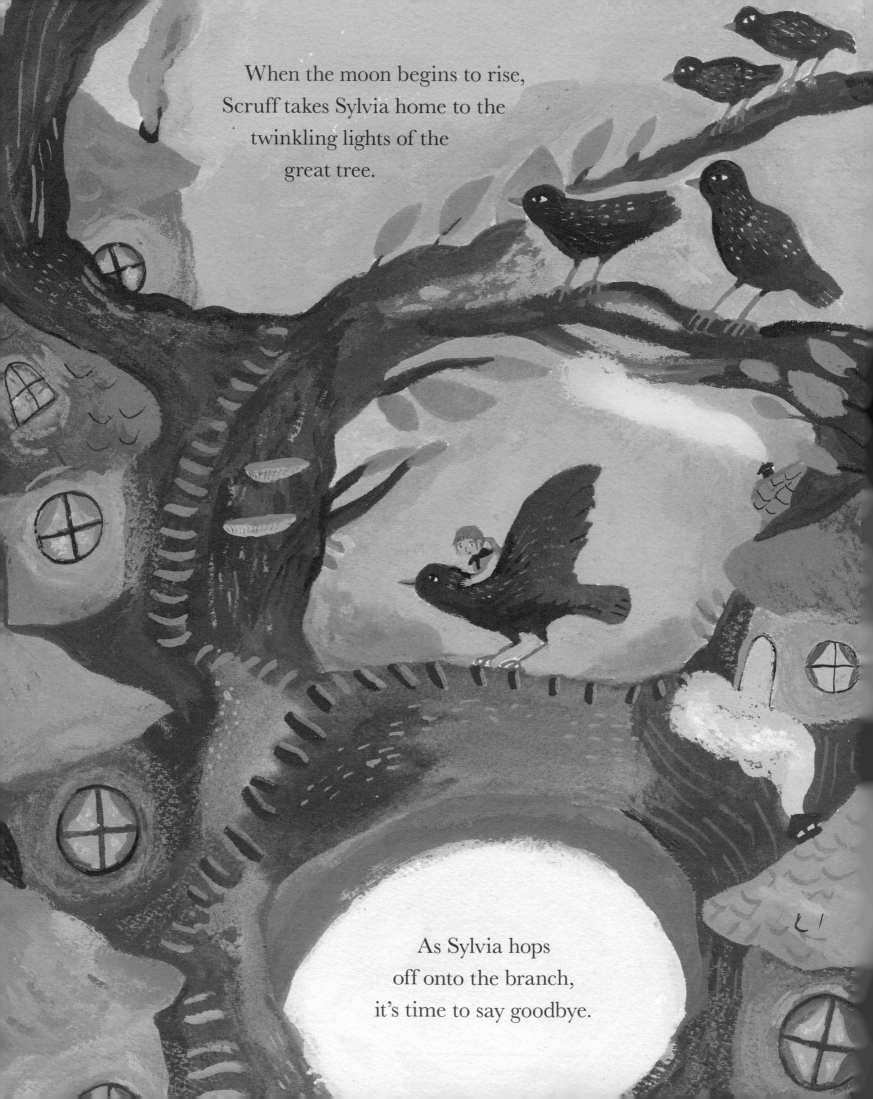

When the moon begins to rise,
Scruff takes Sylvia home to the
twinkling lights of the
great tree.

As Sylvia hops
off onto the branch,
it's time to say goodbye.

Sylvia is very sad.

She knows the flock
is where Scruff belongs…

...but things are too quiet without him.
Her special secret place doesn't feel the same,
and none of the twigs or petals have the
right shape any more.

Then one day,
an acorn rolls down the
stairs towards Sylvia.

"Do you want to
play with us?"
says a girl.

Sylvia thinks about her lonely secret hollow and
about Scruff flying high with the flock. And then
Sylvia, who has always said no before, nods.

As time goes on,
Sylvia finds she likes
playing with the others.

Soon, she has made
many new friends.

In the calm of the den, they stitch garlands
and make stick birds while Sylvia tells
stories of a wild dance in the sky.

Everyone always wants to hear more!

If you peep through the branches of
the great tree today, you'll almost certainly
see Sylvia, leaping, dancing and playing
with friends old and new. Nurture
and mend, gather and tend,

Sylvia is a **Tree Keeper**
and that's what Tree
Keepers do.

About the Author

Gemma Koomen lives in beautiful, wild Northumberland, UK with her husband
and two young daughters. Her love of painting and drawing began as a child when
she spent her days in an imaginary world created with crayons and pencils. She went on
to receive her BFA from Glasgow School of Art. Today, she spends her days making art in
her little studio which, on clear days, looks over wide moors, forests and hills. Inspired by
the simple things in life, Gemma loves time in nature and observing the tiny worlds
that open up when you are quiet enough to notice them. The idea for the Tree Keepers
came from living in a small rural community with close connections to neighbours
and the natural world. *Flock* is her first picture book.